MAHARANA PRATAP

Brishti Bandyopadhyay studied history at St Stephen's College, Delhi. She has written several examination guidebooks for civil service aspirants as well as stories for children for an internet portal.

MAHARANA PRATAP

Mewar's Rebel King

Brishti Bandyopadhyay

RUPA

Published by
Rupa Publications India Pvt. Ltd 2022
161-B/4, Gulmohar House,
Yusuf Sarai Community Centre,
New Delhi 110049

Sales centres:
Bengaluru Chennai
Hyderabad Kolkata Mumbai

The views and opinions expressed in this book are the author's own and the facts are as reported by her which have been verified to the extent possible, and the publishers are not in any way liable for the same.

P-ISBN: 978-81-291-1191-3
E-ISBN: 978-81-291-2661-0

Fifth impression 2026

10 9 8 7 6 5

Printed in India

CONTENTS

THE MEWAR TRADITION

Over 400 years ago, when the glory of the Mughal Empire under Akbar was at its height, a battle was fought near the village of Haldighati in Rajasthan. The mighty Mughal war machine faced the army of the Sisodias of Mewar, a Rajput clan. The Mughals won the battle after a hard-won fight but Rana Pratap, the Mewar King who led the army on the Rajput side, managed to escape. And, for the remaining years of his life, he played a cat-and-mouse game of great inventiveness with Akbar's armies. It made the most powerful monarch of the world vow to use all the resources at his disposal to destroy Rana Pratap. Akbar failed. And Mewar was the only Rajput kingdom to remain free of Mughal domination.

The Rajput clans owed their origins to foreign races like the Hunas and the Sakas. These foreign invaders arrived in

India towards the end of the powerful Gupta dynasty, picked up Indian customs, cultures and modes and marrying locals, merged into the mainstream. They adopted the martial caste of the Kshatriyas as their own and came to be known for their willingness to risk everything, including their lives, for the sake of honour. They were almost always at war with each other or with invading armies from across the Himalayas.

The land, which the Rajputs occupied in northern India, had something to do with the way their personalities were shaped. It came to be known after them—Rajasthan—or the 'abode of the princes'. The Rajasthani terrain offers very little by way of princely comforts, though. The Thar desert lies in the west—stretches upon stretches of golden sand on which beats a relentless sun. The cultivated plains lie in the northeast and the prosperous plateau in the southwest. The Aravalli range of hills stretches from the north to the southeast. At Chittorgarh, Jodhpur and Alwar, the Rajputs dotted the arid, hilly Aravalli landscape with some of the most imposing and magnificent forts and palaces in the world. The hill forts offered superb facilities for military protection against attacks and provided strongholds for organizing defence. The desert helped the Rajputs to hold their own against invaders.

Of all the Rajput kingdoms, Mewar was the most isolated. The Aravallis acted as a barrier, sealing-off Mewar from the rest of Rajasthan.

In ancient times, Mewar was known as Medpat. The

word is said to be connected with Maurya (or More), the Paramara Rajput family, which is the earliest known dynasty to rule in the region. Mewar was the largest kingdom of Rajputana. The hilly regions of the Mewar kingdom were inhabited by the Bhil tribes and the plains by the agricultural communities. Several streams flowing from the hills made the plains fit for agriculture, which served as a granary in times of crisis.

Its geographical seclusion, rugged terrain and harsh physical surroundings made the people of Mewar self-reliant, defensively warlike and stubborn. It also made them develop an intense desire to preserve the glory of their ancestors and their clan, at any cost. They were prepared, mentally and physically, for the kind of protracted hide-and-seek warfare that Rana Pratap would adopt to elude the grasp of a superior Mughal army.

Pratap belonged to an illustrious dynasty that included many legendary personalities. The Rajputs were great fabulists, who loved to invent elaborate myths about their families. Pratap's clan traced its pedigree from mythological times as the descendents of Surya, the Sun God. In reality though, it was Bappa Rawal of the Guhilot Dynasty who in AD 734, established his capital at Chittor and proclaimed himself the ruler of Mewar. The family name changed to Sisodia when Maharana Hamir Singh I from Sisodia mounted the throne.

The Guhilot clan came to Rajasthan from Gujarat and settled down in the southwestern part. They established a stable regime for the next eight centuries and offered resistance to the invading Turks. Jaitra Singh, who ruled from 1213-61, made Chittor the seat of the Mewar government. Chittor was one of the most contested seats of power in India. It is famous in the annals of the Mewar Dynasty as its first capital, and renowned in India as a centre of resistance. The invincible fortress city can be approached only through seven gates of which the topmost was the Ram Pol on the west. Many tanks, constructed on the slopes, assured a permanent supply of water.

The magnificent Chittorgarh fort, crowning a rocky hill, stands near the bank of the river Gambhiri. The length of the fort is about three miles and a quarter and its breadth is a maximum of half a mile. Earlier known as Chitra Durga or Chitrakuta, the fort is believed to have been built by the Rajput Maurya Dynasty in the seventh century AD. It was then named as Chitrakut after Chitrang Mori, a Rajput chieftain as inscribed on ancient Mewari coins. Traditional accounts say that the Mori Dynasty was in possession of the fort when Bappa Rawal seized it in AD 734. Renowned for its strength, the fort was: 'within the grasp of no foe, nor can the vassals of its chief know the sentiment of fear...so intricate are its paths of ascent, that though you might find entrance, there would be no hope of return'.

Being the most important bastion of Rajput power, the occupation of Chittorgarh fort was the primary objective of anyone who wished to establish their rule over Rajasthan. The Rajputs used it as a base to offer a prolonged and determined resistance against invaders from Afghanistan, the Delhi Sultanates and the Mughal Empire. Of the three ferocious sieges that took place for possession of the fort, the first one occurred in AD 1303. The romantic legend of Rani Padmini is linked with this siege.

Padmini was the beautiful princess from Sinhala Dwipa (Sri Lanka), the daughter of King Gandharvasen and Queen Champawati. She came to India to marry the then ruler of Mewar, Rana Ratan Singh. When Sultan Alauddin Khalji of the Khalji Dynasty ruling North India heard about Padmini, he decided to abduct her for his harem. He was also very keen to add Mewar to his empire. He began an attack of the Chittorgarh fort in AD 1302. But after eight months of trying and failing to capture the fort, Alauddin offered to lift the siege on the condition that he be allowed to gaze at Padmini once. Ratan Singh agreed reluctantly. But Rajputs, like Mughals, kept their womenfolk in strict purdah. This meant that Rajput women were kept in seclusion and no outside male was allowed to gaze directly upon them. So, the Khalji sultan had to be satisfied with seeing Padmini's reflection in a mirror in the queen's summer palace. She appeared on the steps of a pavilion in the middle of a lotus pool just across from the palace.

While the Rana was accompanying the Sultan back to the main gates, the perfidious Alauddin offered many apologies for the trouble he had caused. All the while, his soldiers were waiting in ambush just outside the fort's gates. As the huge wooden portals were dragged open, and the Rana was about to bid his adversary a final farewell, the Khalji soldiers pounced upon Ratan Singh and captured him. As ransom for the king, Alauddin demanded that Padmini be turned over to him.

Padmini sent word to Alauddin that she agreed to his demands of ransom. She added that she would be accompanied by seven hundred companions and maids. A procession of palanquins arrived at Alauddin's camp below the fort. All the people accompanying the palanquins, and those inside them, were really armed warriors in disguise. When the right moment came, they burst from the palanquins and attacked. In the battle that followed, Ratan Singh escaped and was escorted back to the safety of the fort. Alauddin went back to Delhi and plotted revenge.

The Sultan was back in January 1303 to lay siege on the fort. The Rajputs resisted for six months, but then the fort's food supplies ran out. Since the fort was situated on a hill surrounded by plains, it was difficult to acquire new supplies. There were only two options left before the proud Rajputs: submit or die. No Rajput wanted to surrender, that left them with death as the only alternative. The Mewar chiefs made a decision, which led to the goriest event in Mewar's history until that time. A huge pile of logs was stacked in the middle of a low-walled, open area of the fort, now called the Mahasati. All of the fort's women, from royalty to maids and villagers, along with their children, took a ritualistic cleansing bath in the nearby reservoir, Gotnukh Kund. The pyre was saturated with ghee and oil, then lit. As the flames roared high into the night sky, the women bedecked in their finest garments and jewels, bid their menfolk a tearful farewell, and began to chant hymns. Then sedated with opium to numb their senses, and led by Padmini, they filed into the Mahasati and leapt on to the pyre, one by one. This horrendous ritual of mass self-immolation, known as jauhar was to be repeated in Rajput history again. The term jauhar is a corruption of Jay Har—meaning Hail Shiva.

With the women and children gone, the men of the fort donned traditional saffron robes of death, threw open the fort's gates, and charged towards the Sultan's army. The Rajputs died to a man. Alauddin emerged victorious, but when he rode inside to claim his trophy, he found that Padmini had cheated him yet again.

Historians say that the character of Padmini has no historical basis. Chittor was conquered for strategic reasons, being on Alauddin's planned route of conquest to southern India. Also, it was too close to the overland trade route from the western seaports to his northern capital of Delhi and to the Muslim holy shrine, the tomb of the Sufi saint Muinuddin Chisti in Ajmer. Jauhar and the final battle did happen though.

Alauddin's armies devastated Chittor and the fort remained in Muslim possession for about ten years until it was retaken by Maharana Hamir Singh I. He was a child who had survived the slaughter, having been sent to safety at Kelwara before Alauddin arrived. It was Hamir who established the Sisodia rule firmly in Mewar and extended the frontiers of his kingdom. His successors Kshetra Singh and Lakha extended the kingdom further. Lakha was a prolific builder who used the wealth of the newly discovered silver and lead mines to rebuild temples and palaces. He also constructed dams to form reservoirs and lakes. The famous Pichola Lake in Udaipur was excavated during his reign.

Rana Kumbha, Lakha's grandson, succeeded to the throne as a boy-king. He embarked on an ambitious project of conquests and expansion of his neighbouring kingdoms. Those who accepted his authority were allowed to retain their land whereas those who did not, saw their kingdoms being snatched. The able conqueror that he was, Kumbha stocked his treasury with the wealth of the conquered kingdoms. The Kirtistambha or Victory Tower in Chittorgarh fort was built by Kumbha to commemorate his victory over Mahmud Khalji, the Sultan of Mulwa.

We now come to Rana Sanga or Sangram Singh, who as grandfather, exercised perhaps the most decisive and enduring influence on Maharana Pratap. A great warrior, Sangram Singh suffered from many physical disadvantages. He was exiled from the kingdom after a fight with his elder brother, Prithviraj, the heir-apparent, during which he lost one eye. He lost an arm in another battle and was crippled by a cannonball in yet another. Altogether, he had eighty wounds on various parts of his body from the sword or the lance. He fought many wars, the most famous one being with Babur in the battle of Khanua.

Babur had invaded India from Kabul and Rana Sangha was determined to throw out this adversary, his resolve bolstered by his initial success against Babur. While he lost a lot of time by waiting, Babur, on the eve of the battle, renounced drinking to inspire his followers.

The deadly conflict, began at about half past nine on 17 March 1527, and went on at such a pitch that the result appeared to be a stalemate. Then, Rana Sanga fainted, having been wounded, and was removed to a safe place. A change of command took place and the artillery power of the Mughals proved to be superior. The loss of life on both sides was terrible. The wounded Rana, on regaining consciousness, heard of the defeat and vowed not to return to Chittor till he had defeated his enemy. He also gave up wearing a turban and began to wrap a cloth around his forehead, instead.

Rana Pratap's father, Udai Singh, was the fourth son of Sangram Singh. Udai was only five when his father died and his eldest surviving brother succeeded to the throne as Ratan Singh II. Two years later, Ratan Singh was murdered and another brother, Vikramaditya, became king. But Vikramaditya had an uncontrollable temper and was a wastrel whose bad behaviour had angered the nobles. So, the nobles appointed a Regent named Banbir, who they felt should rule until Udai Singh reached the age of eighteen and could be appointed ruler.

Banbir however, wanted to become king himself. One

evening in the year 1537, he went, sword in hand, to the harem where Vikramaditya was indulging in his usual merry-making and murdered him. Next, he headed towards Udai Singh's chambers. But Udai Singh's nurse Panna Dai, who had got wind of Banbir's intentions, sacrificed her own child to save the young prince. She smuggled Udai Singh out of the fort and took him on a long and arduous walk to Kumbhalgarh. There, she put him in charge of the local governor, Asha Shah. Meanwhile Banbir, thinking he had killed both Vikramaditya and Udai Singh, declared himself the ruler of Mewar.

Until 1539, the teenaged Udai Singh lived in hiding, passing-off as the Governor's nephew. One day, the chief of Songara, in neighbouring Marwar, visited the fortress. After meeting the seventeen-year-old Udai Singh, the chief was convinced that he was no nephew to the Shah. Rumour quickly spread that the heir to the Mewar throne was still alive. The nobles of Mewar then headed to Kumbhalgarh to confirm the rumour. They interviewed the prince, heard the testimony of Panna Dai and proclaimed Udai Singh their Maharana. After the coronation in 1540, Udai Singh, supported by the chieftains, marched onto Chittor. Banbir too, assembled an army to fight them. They met at Mavli, a town near Chittor, where Banbir was soundly defeated and Maharana Udai Singh II returned in triumph to his capital. It appears that Udai Singh had married while at Kumbhalgarh, since records show that his first son, Pratap, was born there on 9 May 1540.

The first few years of Udai Singh's reign marked a stable period for Mewar because political events beyond its borders were in turmoil. In the north, Mughal rule was interrupted when Sher Shah, who held power in the eastern kingdom of Bihar, defeated Humayun at Kannauj. He established the Sur Dynasty in Delhi and forced Humayun to flee to Persia. It was during this flight that Humayun's son Akbar was born on 15 October 1542. In June 1544, Sher Shah approached Chittor after defeating Raja Maldeo of Jodhpur. Udai Singh, who was in no position to fight the Afghans, sent the keys of the fort to Sher Shah as a token of submission. Sher Shah too, had no desire to embroil himself in yet another war, and signed a treaty with the Mewar ruler. In 1555, Humayun returned to Delhi, defeated Sher Shah Suri and re-established the Mughal rule in Delhi. A year later, he tripped on the steps of his palace library in Delhi, and fell to his death. The accident was concealed for a fortnight to enable Akbar to succeed to the throne peacefully. The new emperor had a grand vision—to bring all of upper India under the Mughal rule.

Akbar embarked upon a series of conquests that saw kingdom after kingdom either fall to his army or acknowledge his supremacy and be allowed to exist as vassal states. He wanted the Rajputs as allies due to their legendary martial spirit, so he married several Rajput princesses. He appointed able Rajputs as generals and soldiers in his army and as ministers in his administration. He abolished two taxes charged on Hindus by earlier Muslim rulers—the pilgrim tax and the jizya. He encouraged both Hindu and Islamic culture and earned the epithet of 'The Great' through his modern and wide-ranging reforms as well as his new approach to governance. In this way he also won over several Rajput kingdoms like Amber, Merta, Gwalior and Marwar.

When Mandu, the capital of Malwa, was stormed, its Sultan, Baz Bahadur, took refuge in Chittor. Though angered by this, Akbar tried diplomacy at first. He sent a peace-keeping mission to Udai Singh suggesting marriage with one of the Rana's daughters. This method of peaceful subjugation through matrimonial alliance had worked with Marwar. It did not work with Mewar as Udai Singh refused matrimonial relations with the Mughals. The emperor then resolved to annex Mewar. Apart from a desire to punish Udai Singh for his defiance, Akbar had a more pressing concern: the Rajput chiefs looked to the Sisodias of Mewar as their natural leaders. If they could be humbled, the other Rajput chiefs too, would submit in fear.

Meanwhile, Udai Singh concluded friendly pacts with Rai Surjan of Bundi and Mansingh Deora of Sirohi and made them his allies. In 1563, he subdued the Rathors of Bhomat and consolidated his position in the south-western part of Mewar. He knew that Mewar needed to be strong to resist Akbar's army.

On 25 October 1567, Akbar pitched his camp below the Chittorgarh fort. In the field, Akbar erected the green flag of Islam, and a pyramidal column, the Chiraghdan or Akbar-ka-dewa (both meaning Akbar's lamp). Formed of large blocks of compact limestone, it had an interior staircase leading to the top. A huge lamp (chirag) was placed on this to denote the imperial headquarters. Udai Singh, meanwhile, called for all the loyal Mewari chieftains to assemble at the capital. He left Chittor in the hands of four Rajput chiefs, Jaimal, Patta, Kalla and Sain Dass, and fled to the town of Girwa.

The fortress of Chittor standing on a hill, towered over the Mughal camp. Its high walls made it difficult to attack. At first, Akbar thought he could never take the fort. It was an immense fortress, well supplied with provisions, wells, and water-tanks, and guarded by eight thousand Rajput warriors. Akbar first tried to take the fort by direct assault which caused a heavy loss of 200 men a day. So, he decided to proceed by means of mines. The Mughals employed cannons to blast holes in the walls. When a part of the wall broke, the Rajputs would repair it at night. In the early hours of 23 February, Jaimal, Udai Singh's general, came to oversee the breach in the wall and was killed by a stray bullet. The Rajputs immediately withdrew from the ramparts and at night the women and children committed jauhar.

A teenager named Patta became the new leader and he charged towards the last battle with his men. Despite putting up a valiant fight, Patta and all his men were killed. Early in the morning, Akbar entered the fortress in triumph and ordered a general massacre 'which ceased only for a lack of victims' in the afternoon, for each bazaar, each street and each house was a fortress and a centre of resistance. Some accounts hold that thirty thousand people were killed in the massacre. The heroism of his adversaries did not go unnoticed by Akbar. He had the statues of Jaimal and Patta mounted on elephants erected at the gate of the Agra Fort. After handing over the reins of Mewar's government to Asaf Khan, the emperor left Chittor for Agra.

Udai Singh has been accused of cowardice by chroniclers because he fled in the face of the enemy. Had he really been a coward, as suggested, he could easily have followed other Rajput princes and accepted subjugation by the Mughals. He chose a strategic retreat instead. Besides, the chiefs of Mewar were adamant that Udai Singh and his immediate family had to quit the fort as preserving the dynastic line was of utmost importance.

Having destroyed Rajasthan's foremost stronghold, Akbar now found it easier to annex the Rajput kingdoms of Jodhpur, Ranthambor, Bikaner and Jaisalmer; the last two even giving their princesses in marriage to Akbar. But while Akbar had conquered Chittor, Maharana Udai Singh and his family were still alive. Mewar was still beyond his reach. So, the emperor chose to wait.

PRATAP TAKES OVER

Udai Singh lived at Gogunda and Kumbhalgarh for brief periods. He made each his makeshift capital until he moved the seat of government to his new capital beside the picturesque Lake Pichola, which he named after himself—Udaipur. He came upon the site of Udaipur by accident. One morning, he was out hunting near Lake Pichola and speared a fast-moving rabbit. All of a sudden, he caught sight of a sage meditating. After paying his respects to the holy man, and recounting the tale of the fall of Chittor, he asked the sage where he should build his new capital. 'Why, right here, of course, where your destiny has brought you to ask such a question,' answered the sage.

Udai Singh ordered the construction of a new palace on the shore of Lake Pichola. Known as the City Palace, the royal abode consists of four major and minor palaces forming a single breathtaking facade overlooking the lake. Built by successive kings after Udai Singh, every addition was beautifully integrated in style and feeling with the existing structures, so as to make the whole seem one. The palace seems to rise from the water and is topped by domes, arches, cupolas, turrets and crenallations. The approach to the palace is through the Hathi Pol (elephant gate) to the north on the main street of the city. The Hathi Pol leads to the Tripolia or Triple Gate of marble arches, right at the spot where Rana Udai Singh speared the hare.

Udaipur was a planned city. Dwellings for nobles and the subjects were constructed near the palace by Udai Singh. The Maharana collected funds, reorganized his army, captured new territories and recaptured many former Mewar provinces. He also organized land reforms and established a new revenue collection system. With the founding of the new city, Mewar became officially known as the Kingdom of Udaipur and Udai Singh, the Maharana of Udaipur. Udaipur flourished to become one of Rajasthan's most charming cities. Its beauty contrasts favourably with the starkness of Chittor. While the rugged fort stands on scrubby country, Udaipur nestles luxuriantly in the lap of the green Aravalli hills.

Tragically, Udai Singh could not enjoy his capital for long. He died at Gogunda in 1572, six months short of his fiftieth birthday. He had been the ruler of Mewar for thirty-five years. Of the twenty-five sons he sired, Crown Prince Pratap Singh was the eldest. Pratap's mother was Rani Jeevant Kanwar, daughter of Akhey Raj Songara Chauhan of Jalore. Like all Rajput princes, Pratap learned the lessons of warfare during childhood. The martial spirit was strong in him and his brothers even as boys. Competitiveness marked his relations with them, especially with Udai Singh's second son, Sakta Singh Kunwar. At age five, Sakta cut his hand on a dagger and revealed that he was fearless. The incident recalled an astrologer's prediction that he would prove to be the misfortune of Mewar. Udai Singh ordered that the child be put to death. But a Choondawat chief of Salumbar (the Choondawats being leading chieftains of Mewar), intervened on Sakta's behalf and offered to adopt the child as he had no heir of his own. Udai Singh approved the request and the chieftain promised to raise the child to be a future leader of the Choondawats. Later, Sakta was sent to attend the royal court and he took his place beside Pratap, the heir-apparent.

The brothers were good friends at first. Gradually though, a growing rivalry was apparent between them. It reached a head one day when, as teenagers, the two brothers were out on a hunting expedition along with the court. Pratap suddenly proposed to end their quarrel by a single combat 'to see who was the best lancer'. As they positioned their horses and took up their lances, the two headstrong boys agreed to charge together. Since this would definitely be suicidal, everyone watched in shock. The purohit or family priest rushed between them and begged them not to do anything that would bring scandal to the House of Mewar. Neither boy was in a mood to listen to the priest's sane advice and adamant about settling their differences there and then. The priest decided there was only one way to prevent the incident. He drew his own dagger and plunged it into his heart. Appalled at the needless death their rash decision had caused, Pratap and Sakta decided not to charge. As a direct result of the incident, Sakta, who was not in his father's good books anyway, was banished from the kingdom. Udai Singh gave him a small force of 200 soldiers and the disgraced youth, burning with resentment against his family, joined Akbar's army.

Pratap, being groomed to be Mewar's next ruler, was now given charge of Mewar's forces. The young commander led the forces to reclaim the kingdom's territories of Chappan and Bhomat. He proved himself to be a man of great courage, foresight, and character; in short, ideal kingly material. He was tall, with a majestic physique—a high forehead, prominent moustaches and bright eyes. Besides the usual princely pursuits, he was also fond of roughing it in the wilds of the Aravalli hills in his youth. Here, he met the local forest-dwellers, the Bhils, and struck up friendship with them. Pratap's wanderings taught him patience, perseverance and courage and, 'an unswerving attachment to its soil, to every shrub and flower that grew there'.

The Bhils are descendants of tribes like the Minas, Meras, Gonds, Abhiras and Gujars who also inhabit the hills and forests of the Vindhya, Malwa and the northwestern Deccan. Called children of the forest, Bhils were the free lords of the jungle, and practised rites and followed customs alien to orthodox Hinduism. They tended flocks and cultivated crops and were famous for their skill in archery. Their language, consisting of numerous dialects, and their religion differed from the Rajputs. They, however, adopted many of the customs and popular mythologies of the Rajputs. On many occasions the Bhils fought wars as bowmen on the side of the princes of Mewar, supplied them with provisions, or guarded the safety of their families when the Mewar warriors went off to battle. The Bhils formed the infantry, attacking the rear and flanks of the enemy, breaking their supply lines and then vanishing quickly to the hills and forests. It was a relationship based on equality.

Nowhere is this special brotherhood reflected better than in the Mewar coat-of-arms: a Mewar Rajput warrior and a Bhil warrior stand on either side of a shield beneath a symbol of the Sun God. It was with these Bhil jungle-dwellers of Central India that the Rajputs established highly enduring alliances. Pratap's was the most celebrated one.

During the third siege of Chittor in 1567, twenty-seven-year-old Pratap offered to lead a force against the Mughals. The nobles were adamant that he should not go. If he died in the siege, they would lose Mewar's only hope for the future. But, as Udai Singh lay dying in 1572, in deference to his favourite queen, Rani Bhatiyani, the Maharana disregarded the tradition of primogeniture. He willed that her son, Jagmal should succeed him. Pratap did not dare resent his father's last wishes and dutifully accompanied the funeral procession at Gogunda, after Udai Singh's death. The heir-apparent, Jagmal remained at the palace. Following the Mewar tradition, he began to ready himself for his imminent coronation.

Mewar's nobles and chiefs had other plans, though. The Choondawat chiefs, known for playing a decisive role in the kingdom's destiny in times of crisis, held a meeting with the other nobles. They noted that the kingdom needed a strong ruler and an able administrator who could hold out against Emperor Akbar who, they knew was going to try and capture Mewar. Rao Akhai Raj of Jhalor, the maternal uncle of Pratap, took the lead. As soon as the cremation was over, they hurried to the palace where Jagmal's coronation had begun. Krishna Das, the leader among the Choondawat chiefs, diplomatically requested Jagmal to step down from the throne. 'You have made a mistake Maharaj,' he said. 'That place belongs to your brother.' When Jagmal refused, the nobles took an arm each and with gentle violence, removed him to a seat in front of the throne. Pratap was carried to the throne amid the cheers of all those who had gathered. After the coronation ceremony ended, there was celebration and feasting. Unable to go against the decision of the nobles, Jagmal seethed with thoughts of revenge. He left Mewar and joined the Mughal forces stationed at Ajmer. Akbar gave him the jagir of Jahazpur. Later, Jagmal was appointed ruler of Sirohi in place of his late father-in-law, Rao Man Singh who had died without an heir. Despite having the help of the imperial forces, Jagmal died fighting Surtan Singh who had been nominated by Rao Man Singh as his successor.

When he became the Maharana of Mewar at the age of thirty-two on 1 March 1572, Pratap inherited the titles and renown of an illustrious house, but was without a capital and adequate resources. At the time of his accession, many important territories of Mewar, including Chittor, were under Akbar's control. But Mewar was still free, as the Mughal king had not been able to force its ruler to accept his imperial authority.

Pratap was imbued with stories of the lost greatness of Mewar and obsessed with a desire to recover its territories, and the fort of Chittor, regarded as the soul of Mewar. He took a vow to reclaim the territories lost to the Mughals, especially Chittor. He found strong supporters of his vow among his chiefs—the successors of Jaimal and Patta, and the chief of Dilwara, among others. At the time of his coronation, Chandrasen, the Rathor chief of Jodhpur, came to visit Pratap. Chandrasen whose kingdom had been seized by Akbar, had pledged undying enmity against the Mughal Empire. One of his daughters was married to Udai Singh. He was warmly welcomed by Pratap.

Pratap decided to take measures that would prepare him and his subjects to face the Mughal army, when it attacked. He moved the seat of government from the scenic Udaipur to the hardier Kumbhalgarh which was home to the second most impregnable fort of Mewar and where he had been born thirty-two years earlier.

Surrounded by thirteen hill ranges of the Aravallis, guarded by seven great gates and seven ramparts, strengthened by rounded bastions and immense watchtowers, the impregnability of the mountain fortress of Kumbhalgarh made it the scene of many battles. A winding road leads through deep ravines and thick forests to the gate Arait Pol with its watchtower. The Badal Mahal Palace is located on top of the fort. Beautiful rooms with pleasant colour schemes of green, turquoise and white in the palace, provide a fascinating contrast to the raw, earthy and grim bastions and walls of the fortress.

With the aid of his experienced chieftains, Pratap remodelled his government, adapting it to the necessities of the time and consolidated his resources. New grants were issued, with regulations defining the service required. Pratap strengthened Kumbhalgarh and Gogunda and other mountain fortresses. His most controversial measure caused his people much hardship and pain: he commanded them on pain of death to retire into the mountains, leaving the fertile tracts they cultivated to become a scorched earth that could not provide sustenance to an invading army.

James Tod, a British Lieutenant-Colonel of the nineteenth century who became an expert on the history of Rajasthan, described the result of this policy in his book, *Annals and Antiquities of Rajasthan*:

'The silence of the desert prevailed in the plains; grass had usurped the place of the waving corn; the highways were choked with the thorny babool, and beasts of prey made their abode in the habitations of his subjects.'

Pratap enforced obedience to this stern policy with

unrelenting severity. He would frequently be seen on his horse, riding to see if his commands were obeyed. One day, he spied a goatherd pasturing his flock in the luxuriant meadows near the bank of River Banas. He ordered the goatherd to be killed and his body hung up to serve as a warning to anyone who dared to disobey. The idea was to render 'the garden of Rajasthan' as Mewar was then called, of no value to the conqueror. He employed bands of mountain warriors to attack Mughal strongholds. They raided goods caravans to intercept the commerce already established between the Mughal court and Europe, which was conveyed through Mewar from Surat and other southern ports. He posted soldiers to guard the Haldighati Pass, the main artery between Udaipur and the north. He also developed his earlier friendship with the Bhils, and hired them as soldiers in his army. The inclusion of the Bhils in the ranks of the Mewar army made possible the guerilla warfare that Rana Pratap adopted after the battle of Haldighati.

Pratap was equally severe on himself and his family. Until victory over the Mughals was achieved, he promised not to eat off gold or silverware but off pattras (plates) of leaves; not to sleep on a bed but on a straw-filled palliasse; and not to shave his beard.

Pratap was a realist who knew that the Rajputs owed their loss of Chittor to their far smaller army, outclassed by weapons and their limited resources. Their age-old strategy of locking themselves up in their inaccessible fortress had proved to be a serious error of judgment in the face of Akbar's clever strategy of encircling the fort, making supply of provisions and reinforcements impossible, his intensive battery charges and mining operations. Their act of throwing open the gates and rushing out at the enemy once their leader was killed may have been very heroic, but it got too many of them killed. A change of strategy was sorely needed and Pratap readied himself for the challenge.

HALDIGHATI AND OTHER WARS

Very soon, Akbar realized that Pratap would never acknowledge the Mughal Empire's superiority. The emperor was not very keen to venture into the treacherous hilly territory of the Aravallis in order to subjugate Pratap either. At the same time, he could not allow the existence of an independent Mewar, a single pocket of resistance to his empire which surrounded it on all sides. Thinking that negotiating a peace treaty might work with the stubborn Maharana, Akbar sent a total of six diplomatic missions to Mewar in 1573. All attempts were unsuccessful, with the Maharana reiterating that he was prepared to sign a treaty with the Mughals only if Akbar acknowledged his sovereignty and Mewar's independence.

Meanwhile, Akbar was aware of another problem. By the end of 1570, he had won over the major Rajput rulers, the Rathors of Jodhpur and Bikaner, the Kachhwahas of Amber and the Bhattis of Jaisalmer. But these rulers secretly admired Pratap's spirit. They had promised their loyalty to the emperor in any future battle. But should Akbar decide to attack Mewar, he was aware that they could forbear from taking up arms against Pratap, who was fast acquiring the cult status of a local hero. Moreover, they were a little embarrassed to be fighting against the house of Bappa Rawal, which they respected. The rulers of Marwar and Amber even sought matrimonial alliances with the House of Mewar, 'to be purified', 'to be regenerated' and 'to be made Rajputs'. On his part, Pratap was equally adamant about not entering into any such alliance with Rajputs who were in the service of the Mughals.

By 1576, Akbar was the wealthiest ruler in Asia and perhaps, Europe. He had a vast empire, a treasury overflowing with riches and the adoration of his subjects. There was no way he could overlook Rana Pratap who was proving to be a thorn in his flesh.

Prince Man Singh of Amber was one of Akbar's most trusted generals and had given his sister in marriage to the emperor. He was the adopted son of Raja Bhagwandas, an influential Rajput leader. Akbar began his overtures by sending Man Singh to Pratap. There were psychological reasons for Akbar's choice of Man Singh too, as Pratap's independence was a standing humiliation to members of the House of Amber. In his time, Kumbha had subjugated the Amber ruler Prithviraj, and forced him to fight under the Sisodia banner.

On his third diplomatic visit to Pratap's camp, Man Singh and Pratap agreed to meet at Lake Udai Sagar, near Kumbhalgarh. A lakeside feast was prepared for the prince. Pratap's eldest son and heir, Crown Prince Amar Singh was summoned to wait upon him; but Pratap himself did not appear. Amar Singh made excuses that his father had a headache and urged Man Singh to partake of the feast. Man Singh refused to eat until Pratap appeared. Then, Pratap did appear and explained that he could not eat with a Rajput who had given his sister to a Mughal and who ate with him as well. Man Singh left the feast untouched and as he was leaving, vowed to humble Pratap's pride and avenge his humiliation. After his departure, the water of the Ganges was sprinkled on the utensils that Man Singh had touched; and the chiefs who had witnessed the incident bathed and changed their clothes, to indicate they were polluted by Man Singh's presence.

All of this was reported to Akbar, who now decided that it was enough and prepared for an all-out war. The emperor blockaded Mewar from the rest of the world and alienated Mewar's traditional allies, some of them Pratap's own kith and kin. Akbar's manoeuvres included trying to turn the people of Chittor district against their king so that they would not help Pratap.

Akbar planned his onslaught of Mewar from Ajmer, where he went to visit the tomb of the Sufi saint, Khwaja

Shaikh Muinuddin Chishti, in early 1576. The massive army that he marshalled included many of his important Rajput allies and minor Rajput chiefs who yielded to the financial temptation and became satraps of Delhi. He made Pratap's arch enemy, twenty-six-year-old Man Singh commanding-general of his troops, telling him to march towards Gogunda and Kumbhalgarh. Akbar then returned to his new capital, Fatehpur Sikri. Akbar's appointment of Man Singh as leader of the Mughal forces was meant to inspire the Rajputs under him to fight with the devotion they may not have shown if they were fighting under a Muslim general. The decision, however, was not popular with the Muslim courtiers, who were resentful of it but Akbar held firm as it was a strategic move on his part.

Records show that Pratap had only twenty thousand soldiers compared to the eighty thousand soldiers of the Mughals. On 3 April 1576, Man Singh left Ajmer at the head of the Imperial Army. He arrived at Mandalgarh in eastern Mewar near Chittor and encamped for about two months. He hoped that Pratap would attack, thus leaving the protection of the hills for the plains where he would be vulnerable in face of the heavy equipment and war elephants of the Mughals. Pratap did no such thing and, instead, left Kumbhalgarh for Gogunda. There, he held a meeting to plan his war strategy. He decided, with his nobles and chieftains, not to fight the enemy on the plains but to lure them into the rugged hills. His plan worked when the Mughal army marched towards the village of Haldighati.

Pratap had taken his position beyond it in the pass (ghati), which could only be reached by a narrow and rugged path about a mile and a half long. A curious feature of the pass is its soft yellow soil which, when crumbled, resembles the spice turmeric (haldi), giving the place its name. The pass ends in a plain where the battle of Haldighati was fought.

The Mewar Rajputs were posted both on the plains and on the cliffs and pinnacles overlooking the field of battle. The Bhils were posted on the cliffs with their bows and arrows, and huge stones ready to be rolled upon the enemy.

The battle of Haldighati was fought on 21 June 1576. Man Singh's vanguard consisted of Rajputs under Jagannath, whereas Pratap's vanguard consisted of Afghan Pathans led by Hakim Khan Sur. The Mughals were waiting on the plains, when Pratap, wearing a helmet and chain armour over a white tunic (still preserved in Udaipur's City Palace Museum), came out and attacked the army. He was astride Chetak, his favourite white stallion and his companion in many decisive battles. Chetak, too, was clad in colourful attire that ended with a mask resembling a grotesque war elephant, designed to terrify an opponent's horse and to protect him from the Mughal war elephants.

In the first flush of attack, Pratap's army almost broke through the Mughal ranks, but they were stopped in time by Man Singh and a few officers. A personal encounter that took place between Pratap and Man Singh, who was riding an elephant, decided the fate of the battle. Pratap heaved his javelin at Man Singh, but ended up killing the mahout, the elephant-trainer. Chetak, who had placed its forelegs on Man Singh's elephant was struck by the sword that the huge beast carried in its trunk. Chetak immediately turned and fled, carrying his wounded master out of danger. Pratap was pursued by two Mughal horsemen but was saved by his brother, Sakta, who had followed them. But having carried his master to safety, his beloved Chetak, who had been severely wounded, died.

The two brothers embraced, the old rivalry forgotten in this hour of peril. Sakta gave Pratap his own horse to ride. They agreed to meet again later, when the opportunity was right. On rejoining Akbar, Sakta narrated a cock-and-bull story that it was Pratap who killed his pursuers and stole Sakta's horse. Naturally, Akbar found it difficult to believe the story. When told that he would be pardoned if he related the truth, Sakta replied, 'The burden of a kingdom is on my brother's shoulders, nor could I witness his danger without defending him from it.' Akbar, though fighting Pratap, was an admirer of the resilience and courage of his arch-foe. He kept his word and pardoned Sakta, but dismissed him from Mughal service.

The battle of Haldighati lasted one day. According to Badauni, one of Akbar's court historians who was present in the field, five hundred soldiers died, of whom 120 were Muslims and the rest Hindus. Many Hindus fought on the side of the Mughals, and it would appear that the casualties on each side were almost equal.

Pratap's sudden withdrawal from the field led to

confusion in the Rajput ranks and the soldiers lost their initial enthusiasm for the fight. By noon, the battle ended in favour of Man Singh. The day was so hot that the Mughals dropped the idea of pursuing the Mewar army. Next day, Man Singh occupied Gogunda, Pratap's temporary capital. The town had already been evacuated. Twenty soldiers, left to guard the palace and the temple, died fighting to save their honour.

The battle of Haldighati has been described as an indecisive battle—an inglorious victory for the Mughals and a glorious defeat for Mewar. It is regarded as one of the kingdom's most memorable episodes as it signalled the beginning of a new type of war—defensive mountain warfare. After retreating into the Aravalli wilderness with his family, Pratap perfected this method of guerilla warfare. He realized that secure makeshift mountain encampments, if properly utilised, could win a small army the battle against a larger, better-equipped force. Haldighati marked a turning point in that Pratap changed his tactics from frontal assault to guerilla warfare, attacking the enemy where and when they least expected it while using the rugged hills as cover.

Pratap launched his guerilla war against Man Singh's army stationed at Gogunda. Fearful of what the wily Mewar ruler might do next, Man Singh barricaded his army with trenches dug around Gogunda and the streets. There were no provisions around Gogunda, as the surrounding countryside was lying desolate. Pratap also cut all lines of communications to Gogunda, and soon the Mughal army was reduced to living on meat and mangoes. Man Singh had no option but to keep his army cooped up within the walls of Gogunda for the three to four months that he stayed in Mewar. So miserable were his soldiers that Man Singh had to send foraging parties to bring whatever food they could find, whether cattle or corn.

Akbar was not satisfied with the results of the battle. He was angry with Man Singh for having abandoned the pursuit of the Rana and so allowing him to remain alive. Later, in September 1576, when he heard of the distressed state of the army of Gogunda, the emperor sent for Man Singh and two other generals, Asaf Khan and Qazi Khan. Accusing them of treachery, he dismissed both Man Singh and Asaf Khan from the court. Man Singh was restored to favour later. Akbar left for Gogunda from Ajmer on 11 October 1576, with a larger army. As soon as he heard of the approach of the Mughal army, Pratap ducked for cover into the hills. Trusted imperial officers like Qutb-ud-din Khan, Raja Bhagwan Das and Man Singh were sent in pursuit to capture him. Narayan Das of Idar, who had joined Pratap's rag-tag group, paid for it when Idar was occupied after a stubborn fight. Pratap also induced Surtan of Sirohi and Raj Khan of Jhalor to join his rebellion.

Akbar came to Mohi near Nathdwara and appointed officers to guard both Nathdwara and Madariya near Chittor. He also appointed officers to guard other Mughal-occupied Mewar territory, 'in order that whenever that wicked strife-monger should come out of the ravines of disgrace, he might suffer retribution'. But the army that was sent against Pratap was unsuccessful, and its two commanders, Qutb-ud-din Khan and Raja Bhagwan Das returned to Akbar who was in Udaipur during this period. They were chastised, then pardoned by Akbar. Soon after, another force was dispatched to Gogunda under Bhagwan Das, Man Singh, Mirza Khan and others as it appeared that Pratap had recaptured Gogunda. The Mughal force recovered the region around Gogunda.

In March 1578, Akbar sent yet another force under the overall command of his foster-brother Shahbaz Khan, to capture the fort of Kumbhalgarh, where Pratap was living. Shahbaz Khan began by occupying Kelwara, a town about three miles from Kumbhalgarh, located at the foot of the mountain. The fort fell after a gallant fight put up by the Rajputs on 3 April 1578, but Pratap eluded capture once more by running away in the nick of time to Chavand in the mountainous area of Chappan, southeast of Mewar. On 5 April 1578, Shahbaz Khan captured Gogunda and at midnight he captured Udaipur.

Shahbaz Khan returned after March 1581 from another campaign, and reported that Pratap's power had been crushed forever.

He was speaking too soon. By the end of 1584, Pratap had succeeded in regaining most of his lost territories, except Chittor, Ajmer and Mandalgarh. Another expedition was sent under Raja Jagannath, but the outcome of the expedition is not very clear. In 1585, Jagannath tried to capture Pratap by surprise in his residence, but Pratap came to know about the plan and fled. Abu'l Fazal the leading Mughal historian and personal friend of Akbar, remarks: 'From foresight the raiding party did not return by the same way, and so proceeded towards Gujarat.' This was probably because the mountain passes and roads, through which the Mughals had to return, were entirely under Pratap's control.

This was practically the last expendition undertaken during Akbar's reign against Maharana Pratap. Akbar gradually became less obsessive about capturing Pratap after this expedition and he turned his imperialist gaze towards Punjab and the Northwest Frontier. For the last ten years of his life, Pratap ruled in relative peace and eventually freed most of Mewar, including Udaipur and Kumbhalgarh, but he could not free Chittor.

Pratap made Chavand his new capital in 1585. He reorganized the administration and founded several new townships and villages. He became a patron of the arts and his reign witnessed the composing of the literary works of *Padmavat Charita* and the poems of Dursa Ahada. Palaces at Ubheshwar, Kamal Nath and Chavand, built in the dense hilly forest, and the temple of Charunda at Chavand, bear testimony to Pratap's love of architecture.

Pratap's valiant and undaunted efforts ensured that most of Mewar remained free at a time when other Rajput kingdoms had fallen victim to Mughal dominance. One day, while hunting, Pratap was seriously injured in an accident. He died at Chavand, aged fifty-six, on 29 January 1597. He was cremated at Bandoli near Chavand where a cenotaph built in his honour still exists. Akbar died eight years later.

FINALE

Pratap's life and times are known to us through three main sources, the official history of the Mughal period written by court historians, the Rajasthani chroniclers, and, Tod's *Annals and Antiquities of Rajasthan.* The Mughal historians, Abu'l Fazl and Badauni, wrote of Rana Pratap as a renegade and a troublemaker who caused Akbar many difficulties due to his refusal to accept Akbar's sovereignty and to become an ally of the Mughals. The Rajasthani chroniclers, including bards who composed heroic verses, regard him as the greatest hero of medieval India and the bravest of Rajputs. It is a view that is corroborated by Tod's account of the exploits of the warrior-king. Tod's book is regarded as a storehouse of material dealing with various facets of Rana Pratap's life not usually found in historical works.

All three sources shed valuable light on the type of man that Rana Pratap was and what compelled him to act the way he did. The exploits of Rana Pratap narrated by the bards and Tod combine myth with legend and make for fascinating reading. Both relate romantic tales of a ruler made penniless and his sturdy frame exhausted by years of fighting, all because of his refusal to surrender his freedom. His family was Pratap's chief source of anxiety as he dreaded their captivity. On one occasion, faithful Bhils saved the women and children by carrying them in wicker baskets and concealing them in mines, where they guarded and fed them. Witnessing sons and relatives, his bravest nobles and many of his faithful subjects die on the battlefield made him acutely aware of his misfortunes. He was often heard to say, 'For this the Rajput was born.'

A favourite tale of the bards is the one where a despondent Pratap, after years of fighting Akbar, sent a note to the emperor demanding an end to his ordeal. An overjoyed Akbar, who thought that this meant submission, showed the letter to a Rajput at his court, Prince Prithiraj, the younger brother of Rai Singh, who was the ruler of Bikaner. Astonished and grieved by the decision, Prithiraj told Akbar that the letter was a forgery of sorts as he was sure that Pratap would never submit to the emperor's terms. He requested and obtained the emperor's permission to send a letter to Pratap. He told Akbar this was to ask Pratap the reason for his submission, but his real purpose was to prevent it. He wrote, 'The hopes of the Hindu rest on the Hindu; yet the Rana forsakes them. But for Pratap, all would be placed on the same level by Akbar; for our chiefs have lost their valour and our females their honour. Akbar is the broker in the market of our race: he has purchased all but the son of Udai (Singh II of Mewar); he is beyond his price. What true Rajput would part with honour for nine days (nauroza); yet how many have bartered it away? Will Chittor come to this market...?' The highly emotional content of the missive had its effect on Pratap, who decided against submitting.

But the effect of holding out against the Mughals took its toll on Mewar. The kingdom was devastated by a decade of constant fighting and deliberate destruction by the Mughal army and, Pratap's stern order against cultivating the land. A large number of people also died of hunger, malnutrition and disease as a result of the war, and many peasants left Mewar and settled in other peaceful neighbouring regions. These effects mainfested themselves keenly during the reign of Pratap's son, Amar Singh.

Pratap had eleven queens and Amar Singh was the eldest of his seventeen sons. Amar had to fight the Mughals and at the same time maintain a stable administration that would provide him the means to carry on the struggle for freedom. He began by introducing certain necessary administrative reforms meant to reduce the growing power of the nobles in his court. Tod has graphically described the nomadic wanderings of a penniless Pratap following the battle of Haldighati. But this is more fiction than fact. Not only did Pratap have enough financial resources to carry on the struggle, he ensured that Amar Singh, too, was not short of funds. Pratap's judicious use of the wealth that had been hoarded in the treasury by Kumbha and Sanga allowed his son to continue fighting the Mughals till 1614.

Maharana Amar Singh fought several wars with the Mughals, the first one in 1600, when Akbar sent an army under Crown Prince Salim and Man Singh. But Salim failed to accomplish anything due to his indolence, remarks Abu'l Fazal, and rebelled soon after. He reconciled with Akbar and, in October 1603, was sent from Agra at the head of a well-equipped army. This venture, too, was abandoned by the wayward Salim. Finally, Akbar appointed Kunwar Sagar Singh, a younger brother of Pratap, to rule the conquered territory, but he died before he could make Sagar the Rana.

Salim, who after succeeding Akbar, became Jahangir, sent his son Parviz to conquer Mewar. He told Parviz to talk peace with Amar Singh only if the Rana or his eldest son, Kama Singh, came to wait upon him. But rebellions were breaking out and Parviz agreed to Amar Singh's condition to send Bagha Singh, a younger son of Amar to Jahangir's court.

Nothing much happened as a result of the visit. It was only in 1614, that Prince Khurram, Jahangir's heir-apparent who became known as Shah Jahan later, achieved some success against Amar Singh. By now, the condition of the Mewar army was really bad with an acute shortage of provisions and weapons. The proverbial last straw that broke the Mewar camel's back was Khurram's inhuman practice of making prisoners of women and children. Fed up, the nobles came to Prince Karna one day. They had been fighting for forty-seven years, were without food, dress or even weapons and now had to bear the indignity of seeing their children being captured by Mughals and forced to become dancing girls or slaves. While preserving the honour of the state, they were forced to endure the loss of the honour of their families. The nobles urged Karna to come to some sort of agreement with the Mughals. Karna agreed with the nobles, but he was afraid his father would not. So he sent two nobles, Subhakarna and Jhala Haridas to Khurram without letting Amar Singh know about it.

Khurram sent the two Mewar envoys to Ajmer where Jahangir and the emperor issued a farman or royal letter with the mark of his plan. Khurram sent the farman to Amar Singh who, by now, had come to know about the secret negotiation and accepted the terms. On 18 February 1614, Amar Singh visited Khurram and gifted him a large ruby and seven elephants. Not to be outdone, Khurram gifted Amar Singh a superb dress of honour, a jewelled sword, a jewelled saddle, and a private elephant with silver housings. After Amar left, Prince Karna arrived at Khurram's camp and the two started for Ajmer. Jahangir received Karna with graciousness and overwhelmed him with gifts and attention. Jahangir's chief queen, Nur Jahan, gifted Karna a rich dress of honour, jewelled sword, a horse and saddle, and an elephant. Karna left Jahangir with his son Jagat Singh, then a boy of twelve.

Amar Singh regained all of Mewar and Chittor. The

only restriction to his sovereignty was that the fort of Chittor could not be repaired. He was also required to send a contingent of troops to the Mughals, but he rarely did so. In order to retain the independence that his father had fought so hard for, he gained the much-needed peace to restore the ravaged Mewar to some semblance of civilized existence. Would Pratap have accepted this treaty? Then again, would Akbar have offered such terms? We do not know. It is true, though, that the land between Chittor and Udaipur was soaked with the blood of Mewar and Mughal heroes. By now, both sides were tired of fighting and eager to come to terms.

However, Amar Singh was so insulted at having been forced to accept the Mughal farman that he retired to his private chambers leaving Mewar's administration in the hands of Karna Singh. He may have been reminded of the misgivings of Pratap just before his death, that Amar would not have the stomach for carrying on the struggle the way he, Pratap, did. He died on 26 January 1620.

All of Karna's energy were spent in restoring the fortunes of a war-devastated Mewar. He maintained cordial relations with the Mughals under Shah Jahan, even helping the emperor during his rebellion when still a prince in 1622. Following Karna's death in 1628, the two sides maintained an uneasy truce, with some friction arising due to the Mewar rulers' attempts to repair the Chittor fort. Within a few years of Emperor Aurangzeb's accesion to the throne however, Mughal-Mewar relations took a turn for the worse.

Aurangzeb, who was a strict Muslim, lacked the enlightened views that had governed Akbar's approach to the Rajputs in particular and his Hindu subjects in general. He reimposed the jizya tax and demanded that Raj Singh, the ruler of Mewar, impose it in his kingdom. He also destroyed a few of the famous temples of Rajasthan and carried the images to Delhi where they were placed before the mosques as steps, so that faithful Muslims on their way to prayer, might tread on them. However, it was the Rathor state of Marwar that Aurangzeb wanted to annex, causing much tension to Raj Singh as annexing Marwar would enable the Mughals to outflank the country and enter Mewar through the Aravalli passes. A Sisodia-Rathor alliance was the only answer to check Aurangzeb's bid to capture the kingdoms. After Aurangzeb had captured Jodhpur, the Marwar capital, the Rathors who were guided by a brave noble Durga Das shifted their base of operations to Mewar. Auranzeb sent stern letters to Raj Singh demanding that he turn over Ajit, the minor prince of Jodhpur who had sought refuge in Mewar, to the Mughals. True to the Sisodia tradition, Raj Singh refused and supported Durga Das in his guerilla warfare against the imperial army. Later, on 24 June 1681, a peace treaty was signed between the Mughals and Jay Singh who took over the administration of Mewar from Raj Singh. The war in Marwar continued for thirty years.

His successors and other Rajput states continued to be inspired by Rana Pratap's example long after he died. For twenty-five years, Pratap had dared to defy the wrath and might of the greatest Mughal, Akbar. His refusal to submit to Akbar led to the devastation of large parts of Mewar under a series of do-or-die expeditions, and the depletion of the treasury had caused great suffering to his people. Yet, unlike his contemporaries, Rana Pratap chose a life of adversity as a rebel over a life of leisure as a Rajput in the Mughal court. If Akbar had intelligent and able Rajputs under his command, Pratap too, built up coalitions to stem the tide of Mughal power in Rajasthan. He inspired the chiefs of Idar, Sirohi, Dungarpur and Banswara to defy Akbar, even after their kingdoms had been taken over by the Mughal forces. His strategy of guerilla warfare exploited in full the geographical advantage of the hills and ravines. It was from him that another guerilla leader learnt the strategy of evading the forces of Aurangzeb in the Deccan. This was the Maratha, Shivaji, of the seventeenth century. Much later, in the twentieth century, Bengal revolutionaries fighting British rule would also draw inspiration from Pratap's relentless struggles against the Mughal empire.

The conflict in Mewar between Rana Pratap and Akbar can be regarded as a contest between two extraordinary minds. One bent on establishing a pan-India empire, and the other, equally determined to preserve the autonomy of his small principality. What makes the conflict so fascinating and replete with romance, valour and intensity, was that both sides were represented by two of the most interesting personalities of the sixteenth century. Even though Akbar brought to the conflict all the vast resources and the best military talent he had at his command, he could not bring about the subjugation of one kingdom and its defiant ruler. Rana Pratap, while he had the satisfaction of never bowing to Mughal might, was left with the sadness of not being able to regain his beloved Chittor in his lifetime. The contest involved conflicting ideologies. One held by an outstanding emperor who desired an empire spanning all of India under his central authority and, the other by a brilliant guerilla fighter and proud ruler who would try everything he could to preserve his kingdom's independence.

BIBLIOGRAPHY

The Mughal Empire	Bharatiya Vidya Bhavan
Ain-i-Akbari	Abu'l Fazl
A Comprehensive History of India	People's Publishing House
Annals and Antiquities of Rajasthan	James Tod
Akbar	J.M. Shelat

CHRONOLOGY

9 May 1540

Born at Kumbhalgarh, eldest son of Udai Singh II and Rani Jeevant Kanwar.

Named Pratap Singh.

1540

Udai Singh, fourth son of Maharana Sangram Singh I and Rani Karmavati, crowned Maharana of Mewar.

15 October 1542

Akbar born to Humayun and Hamida Bano.

14 February 1556

Akbar becomes ruler of Mughal empire.

October 1567

Akbar encamps with this troops in front of Chittorgarh fort, after

Udai Singh refuses diplomatic overtures.

February 1568

Siege and fall of Chittor. Udai Singh flees to Girva.

1572-1576

Udai Singh dies at Gogunda. Pratap Singh crowned and becomes Maharana Pratap.

Undertakes remodelling of government and begins planning war strategy.

1573

Akbar sends six diplomatic missions to Mewar. All fail.

3 April 1576

Akbar announces Man Singh's appointment as the commander of the expendition to Mewar from Ajmer.

April-June 1576

Man Singh's army encamps at Mandalgarh.

21 June 1576

Battle of Haldighati. Mughals win the war, Pratap escapes.

1576

Pratap launches guerilla war against the Mughals, using the hills for cover.

11 October 1576

Akbar leaves Ajmer for Gogunda. Narayan Das of Idar, Surtan of Sirohi and Raj Khan of Jhalor join Pratap's army.

3 April 1578

Shahbaz Khan captures the fort of Kumbhalgarh. Pratap still at large.

1584

Pratap regains most of his lost territories, except Chittor, Ajmer and Mandalgarh.

1585

Pratap founds new capital at Chavand.

29 January 1597

Pratap dies after being wounded in a hunting accident.

1597

Amar Singh, eldest son of Pratap, becomes Maharana.

February 1614

Amar Singh signs peace treaty with emperor Jahangir, bringing the Mewar-Mughal war to an end.